ALSO BY TORREY MALDONADO

What Lane?
Tight
Secret Saturdays

HANDS

TORREY MALDONADO

 Nancy Paulsen Books

NANCY PAULSEN BOOKS

An imprint of Penguin Random House LLC, New York

First published in the United States of America by Nancy Paulsen Books,
an imprint of Penguin Random House LLC, 2023

Copyright © 2023 by Torrey Maldonado

Visit us online at penguinrandomhouse.com.

Library of Congress Cataloging-in-Publication Data
Names: Maldonado, Torrey, author.
Title: Hands / Torrey Maldonado.
Description: New York: Nancy Paulsen Books, an imprint of
Penguin Random House LLC, New York, 2023. |
Summary: Twelve-year-old Trevor has an adult problem to deal with: how to protect
himself, his sisters, and his mother from his abusive stepfather (currently in prison) and he
thinks the way to do that is to take up boxing—although he would really rather draw.
Identifiers: LCCN 2022036081 | ISBN 9780593323793 (hardcover) |
ISBN 9780593323809 (ebook)
Subjects: LCSH: Stepfathers—Juvenile fiction. | Families—Juvenile fiction. |
Responsibility—Juvenile fiction. | Boxing stories. | CYAC: Stepfathers—Fiction. |
Family life—Fiction. | Responsibility—Fiction. | Boxing—Fiction.
Classification: LCC PZ7.M2927 Ha 2023 | DDC 813.6 [Fic]—dc23/eng/20220816
LC record available at https://lccn.loc.gov/2022036081

Printed in the United States of America

ISBN 9780593323793
2nd Printing

LSCH

Edited by Nancy Paulsen
Design by Cindy De la Cruz
Text set in Ten Mincho and Autumn Voyage

Ma, you almost lived to hold *Hands* in yours.
I love and miss you.

CHAPTER 1

YOU promise? I promise. People say people have "promise." Whatever that means.

All I know is . . . I got promises to keep. I *have* to. But which ones are right? Which are wrong?

Messed-up stuff happened with my stepdad. Has me feeling messed up. Feeling torn and confused about what to do.

I thought my stepdad was the Man. Tried to make him smile. Hoped he'd accept me. Needed to be his boy after my pops died. Wanted to be *his*. Followed him.

But not no more. *Nah.*

Not after that night he got locked up for throwing hands. And not with just anyone . . .

CHAPTER 2

YOU don't mess with my mother.

But my stepdad did.

I only saw him hit her that one night.

My mom shielded me *a lot* after my real dad died when I was seven. I guess she couldn't shield me completely because my dad dying hurt so bad I got left back. It's why I'm now twelve in the sixth grade.

Ma was hyped my stepdad wanted her: a woman with two kids. He promised to protect her, and us. He had his own kid, my stepsister, Jess.

My sister and stepsister are my hearts. My stepsister, Jess, is the oldest, seventeen. My sister, Nikki, is fifteen.

Real fast, my mom and stepdad started living together, and real fast, talking about my real dad stopped because my stepdad wanted to be the *only* man of the house. He didn't want to hear anything about my pops.

Here's how I know.

Once, me and my stepdad walked to the store and

passed a couple of grandma-aged women on a bench. One friendly-shouted, "Hey, Spider-Man!"

I knew she was talking to me because I had on a Miles Morales Spider-Man T-shirt. Back then I was into-into Miles's Spider-Man. He's still fire.

She waved at me. "Boy, you Trevor?"

I nodded.

The woman next to her elbowed her and smiled. "Brenda, you *know* that's Trevor Junior. Same handsome face as his father's." She eyed my stepdad. "No disrespect. You cute, but his real dad was *fi-iine*."

She didn't mean to be rude, but my stepdad's face got tight how people's faces do when a splinter pricks their finger bloody.

I wanted to stay getting props for looking like my real pops and being told how dope he was, but my stepdad put his hand on my back and interrupted the women. "We gotta go."

The first woman who spoke—Brenda—called out to my stepdad's back as he shoved me forward. "Hope you a gentleman like Trevor's dad! That man was such a gentle—"

My stepdad shooed me with more force, and then half a block away, he told me, "You be *lucky* if you look like *me*. But enough talking about your old man."

So anyway, back to the night my stepdad got arrested,

he got heated because *he* got himself two more years in jail for violating his parole.

I was shocked he blamed Ma for everything.

Jess and Nikki were shocked too—shocked that I was surprised at what he did. They said the same thing: "Trev, we need to talk. There's a lot you don't know."

What didn't I know?

And how'd I miss it?

CHAPTER 3

AS cops put my stepdad in their car, he shouted at Ma like he was making a promise. "I'll get you back! YOU did this to me! YOU got me locked up!"

How was it her fault? *He* hit her. *He's* wrong.

And what'd she do anyway?

Later that night, Jess and Nikki tell me more. What I missed. Turns out Ma did nothing to get hit because nothing ever deserves getting hit.

They came in my room and our whole conversation was whispers.

Me: "Did he always hit her?"

Jess: "No. They'd just argue."

Nikki: "Ma used to win, nonstop."

Jess: "Facts."

Nikki: "Until that day he—"

Me: "What?"

Jess: "Ma said he shook a fist near her face. Threatened to clock her. And threatening became his thing when he couldn't win with words."

"He ever put his fist in your faces?" I ask.

Jess: "No! Ma wouldn't let him. She said she'd die before she let that happen!"

Jess shares why the big fight started. "They were arguing about you, Trev. Dad told Ma, 'You raising him *soft*.' I know because I'd eavesdrop at their bedroom door when they argued. Dad barked, 'I tried teaching him to box and he was all whiny. *No. I don't want to throw a punch. I don't want to hurt anybody.*'" Jess eyes me now. "Did that really happen?"

I feel guilty and nod. "Yeah."

Jess sucks her teeth. "Anyway. Their fight got louder—and I don't know why, but he snapped. He must've lifted his fist because she said, 'I'm NOT scared of YOU.' Then *BOOM!* Everything went *too* quiet."

I think back to the cop car, to my stepdad's promise that he'd get her back for calling the cops on him.

And that night, as Ma iced her puffy eye, I made a promise through my salty tears, deep in my heart:

On my life . . .

On my mom's . . .

On my sisters' . . .

He won't *ever* hit Ma again.

Never.

Watch.

CHAPTER 4

AFTER my stepdad got taken away, the nightmares began. In them, he'd stand over Ma, pumping his fist near her face.

> I yell, "STOP!!!"
> He turns and grins at little me. "What you gonna do?"
> His grin grows into a snarl as he steps closer.
> Teasing me: "What? You? Gonna? Do?!"

I'd wake up. Punching, kicking, trying to knock his grin off his face.

I had to do something. So I did what I saw Muhammad Ali, Mike Tyson, Creed, Floyd Mayweather, and Jake Paul do in old clips online. I got on the floor and did push-ups and sit-ups until my body shook and my heart pumped different. Wild, unstoppable thumps. Felt less helpless, less scared.

Amped, I stood and threw a punch, huffing. "I'm Ali."

Then I threw a flurry of punches, each time saying the boxer I pretended to be.

"I'm Creed."

"I'm Tyson."

"I'm Mayweather."

I didn't worry about hurting anyone anymore like when my stepdad tried training me. Nope, not when it was him I imagined I was hurting and stopping from hitting Ma.

From my mirror, I saw my muscles get more pumped. I felt more swole, jacked. Like the superheroes I used to draw.

And I grew mad tall. In the two years since my stepdad's been gone, I've shot up two feet. I'm twelve now and almost six feet tall. Lots of people think I'm in high school. Tall people out here tell me, "When'd you get my height?"

"Gentle giant," Ma likes to say. She always winks at me when she says it. She likes the "gentle" part.

Gentle? I used to be that. Am I still that?

It's just I can't be gentle if my stepdad flips on Ma again when he's back.

Giant—that's what I need to be to protect her. More diesel, stronger.

Sometimes, though, I wonder, *What if Ma never met him? Who'd I be?*

CHAPTER 5

"DON'T let no one mess with your sisters. Stand up for them. Protect them, no matter what." My stepdad made me promise that once when we were out and saw a teenage guy grip his girlfriend's wrists and shake her.

"How do I protect my sisters?"

He lifted his fists. His knuckles were cracked red. "With these. *Promise.*"

I looked at my baby-soft knuckles. My sisters could probably beat me up, but he poked me in the chest. "Agree?"

So I did. "I promise."

But what about him?

I should've made him promise too. What happens when the one who's supposed to have your back is the one you need protecting from? It messes you up. Makes you walk east and west at the same time.

That tears you up.

It tears something in you.

Makes me want to tear him up.

CHAPTER 6

ME and my boy Pete—P—met last summer, when he moved into my building and I saw him in our hall speaking nice to Little Cole.

Little Cole is eight and lives in the apartment across from me and reminds me of little me. Our hall is maybe the safest in our projects. Some halls you better not pass through. Mine? Library quiet and chill. I learned that when I was Cole's age and went to throw trash in our hallway incinerator. The trash chute swallowed the garbage bag real loud—*SWOOSH*—then the whole world got silent. "Hey?" My voice echoed down the hall, but nobody answered. Right then, I rushed in and asked Ma, "Can I sit in the hall and draw?" She smiled. "Sure. But come in if you get uncomfortable."

So, for a few years our hall was my paradise and now it's Little Cole's. When he's there, I'll ask, "You good?" and might sit and listen to him draw and ramble.

"You see this?" Little Cole said once, and pointed at his drawing.

"Yeah."

"It's a portal. Ask me where it goes."

"Where's it go, Cole?"

"If we stepped in it—*fwoosh*—we'd zap into another universe. To a place where I can swim better than Aquaman—even in the deepest ocean . . ."

His imagination makes me smile. Makes me wish I could be like him again.

That day I met P, I'm peeking through my peephole and see a guy around my age who's kneeling next to Little Cole. I almost rushed out there—big brother protective—but Cole giggled and dude's body language seemed safe, cool. I strained to eavesdrop. Stranger-dude's eyes popped and I heard him say, "Wooooow. You draw better than me and I'm older than you. I just moved here today."

"I can teach you to draw," Little Cole said.

The guy nodded. "Then you my first friend in this building."

Little Cole pointed at my apartment. "My friend Trevor lives there. He says I'm a master artist."

I figured it was a good time to come out and opened my door. "Hey, Cole. You out here making friends?"

I stepped to this new guy with my hand out. "I'm Trevor."

He reached back and we dapped.

"Call me P. Short for Pete."

From the jump, we clicked. And right then to now, our first hi turned into secret handshakes and I learned a lot about P.

CHAPTER 7

P'S adopted and has no sisters or brothers. He feels alone, stays alone. I get him on that. I like to stay mostly alone too. Can't explain it. We don't make friends easy. Because who's real? Who's fake?

Me and him? We brothers. Might as well be. Almost everything the same—skin color, humor . . .

One morning, we in his apartment when he points at a pile in his living room. "My pop's tossing that out. Even them boxing gloves. Pads too."

"Nah, save those," I said. "We'll use 'em."

"Word?"

"*Word.*"

Same day, we started boxing in the stadium across the street from the rec center. The stadium stays mostly empty. It's got some grassy baseball fields, tennis courts, and a track that people and school teams who aren't from here jog on.

Tap-tap-tap. At first, I hit P's pads like that.

Then, *bap-bap-bap.*

"Harder!" P grunts at me.

I think of my stepdad and imagine his face on Pete's pads, grin-snarling at me. I unload—*Blat! Blat! BLATTITY-BLATTITY-BLAT-BLAT!*

I notice P's eyes pop. He's surprised by my strength but squats down to brace himself to see if I can add more to my punches. He barks, "Harder."

I nod, picturing my stepdad's face again, and swing with everything.

P backs up and pulls a pad off and shakes pain out of his red palm. "You a monster."

Nah. He's wrong.

He don't know the real monster is about to come out.

CHAPTER 8

MA keeps a photo on her night table of her and my stepdad at Old Timers' Day, and it makes me remember then, when he was cool.

Old Timers' Day is in summer when folks who once lived here link up with people who still do in the park. Mad cookouts, music, and chilling. At that Old Timers' Day, my mom and stepdad sat on a bench and fed each other forks of barbecue. You'd think it was just them two in the whole park when maybe a thousand people were around them.

I start thinking of other times he treated her right.

She'd work late and come home tired and he'd tell her, "Sit," and he'd make dinner for us. She needed to shop and he'd say, "I'll go," and he did. Sometimes, he'd even sit with me and help me figure out my homework.

But now? How can she keep a photo of him next to her bed? How she still love him?

Her loving him makes me start to feel like . . .

. . . if she thinks he's not *so* bad . . . then *maybe* . . .

. . . *maybe* things aren't *so* bad? Maybe . . .

. . . he's not so bad?

Does her loving him mean maybe I'm supposed to love him too?

I'm so confused, so east and west. Torn in two.

CHAPTER 9

TODAY, me and P are in the stadium having fun because P has us try new punching combos.

I huff, then catch my breath. "Where you learn these moves?"

"Some videos last night. Let's do Mike Tyson. I'll throw a left jab. You duck under. Step in. Right uppercut. Left uppercut."

I nod. "How many times?"

"Till it sounds like music. Tyson had this rhythm, *Duck-bap-bap. Duck-bap-bap. Duck-bap-bap.* Ready?"

He jabs, and I go for it.

"Nah," P says, "you in too close. No power in your punches. Try again."

P jabs.

I go hard, swinging better. *Duck-bap-bap. Duck-bap-bap.*

He smiles, and says, "You getting the rhythm. Speed up."

It's like a video game: Master one level, things get quicker.

P: *Jab.*

Me: *Duckbapbap. Duckbapbap. Duckbapbap.*

P laughs. "Bruh, now you *too* fast."

We keep it up. Smiling, swinging. Getting the rhythm.

We go until we can't no more. Then at the same time we fall down on each other, tired-laughing.

"Whooo," he exhales.

"BRUH!" I gasp.

We crawl to our backpacks and sit-lean on the fence that circles the track. Our shoulders touch. The sun sets and our bodies glow from it.

He sips his OJ, then passes me it.

"Who nice with hands like we tryna be?"

I swig. "Why?"

"Kinda like a high score. We can't reach the score if we don't know it. Have a goal, y'feel me?"

"Facts."

"So?" He takes his OJ back. "Who?"

"Well, when I was ten, I got jumped by ten guys."

P's shocked. "Word?! Who?"

"Classmates from back then."

"Who?"

"Don't matter. So five really punched, kicked me. The other five stood lookout and hyped them up. Just because my boy Chris got mad his girl said I was cute. Pretty sure she only meant I was a cute little kid because I was just ten."

"Five-on-one is foul!" P says. "Bet none had the heart to fight one-on-one."

"True—and some I thought were my boys. But they wanted to prove they were *really* Chris's boys. Happened after school as I walked alone. When Chris jumped in my face, I heard Ma's voice in my head, *Just apologize. It'll calm him down.* But that only works sometimes—it didn't work at all for her with—"

"With who?" P asks.

"Never mind." I don't want him knowing too much of my business. I keep on. "All I could do after they beat me was run mad fast toward our projects. Them chasing and whaling on me. Two blocks from my building they stopped. I guess they figured it's my turf and heads'll have my back. And my stepdad's friends did: 'Ayo, that's Trev!' They pointed to me. Jumped off benches. Flew off stoops. Ran toward us. The kids who'd jumped me jet.

"When I get home, my stepdad sees me and loses it. 'YO! Your face!' I told him I was okay. Said I wanted to forget the whole thing. Not him. 'Tomorrow, I'm coming to your school, after school. And you better point each boy out. And you gonna fight each one.'"

P's eyes bulge. "Did you?"

"Did I what?"

"Fight all five heads?"

"Nah. You right. None of them wanted a fair one. Good thing since I doubt I coulda even fought back then. But they saw me with my stepdad, got scared, and left."

For a moment, I remember Ma's reaction when my stepdad was all hyped-happy how he pushed me to fight. "You're proud of that? You think fighting solves anything? Do you know where it leads? To more fights. To trouble with police. You want that for Trevor? Or something worse?!"

P pulls me out of that memory. "Well, at least your pops has heart. He must be mad nice with hands."

"I guess you could say that." I tell P about the time he beat up three guys all at once—how guys on TV or in movies do—but I say it how it happened and not to make P think I'm big-upping my stepdad, which I'm not.

CHAPTER 10

"I guess sometimes you just gotta throw hands." P shrugs.

"Facts."

"Solves stuff. Some cats don't get it, till they get hit."

"Yeah." Him saying that makes me wonder, *Does it have to be this way? All the time?*

P counts fingers like he's reciting some equation. "Throw hands. Dude feels your power. He gets the message. He stops playing. No one else gets involved. Problem solved. How your dad did."

I think of my stepdad. Guess I never realized that's how he solved stuff, with hands.

P interrupts my thinking. "Your pops on that next level. He's the Man."

"Why?"

"Cuz everything you just said."

I want to say what he did to Ma. But that's not how you do fam. She raised me to not bad-mouth them.

P keeps on. "*And* he shoots fair ones, right? Don't use weapons."

Now I wonder more. *Can I say my stepdad won't ever use something? He sometimes carries—*

P interrupts my thinking again. "Where he at?"

"Jail."

"What? Thought you said he moved Down South."

Ugh. I didn't mean to tell the truth just now. He caught me in that lie. Oh well.

"Yeah, P. I lied about it back in the day because I was embarrassed."

"Don't be. So many people have family locked up. Plus I'm your boy. He's in for fighting?"

Now P's all questions and I wish I would've shut up a while ago. "Yeah," I say.

He apologizes like people do a lot when they learn where my stepdad is.

"C'mon." I stand up. "Put pads on."

"Thought we done."

"Nah, P. Gotta get on my pop's level."

He stands, slides pads on, and holds up his hands.

"You think you got what he has?"

"Hope so—if I gotta solve stuff with my hands."

CHAPTER 11

COULDN'T go anywhere with my stepdad without hearing it.

"You and your pops got the same walk."

"Dang. Same tall height."

"Be a good son."

Back then I liked it. Now the thought of them saying we similar is mad annoying.

He. Is. Not. My. Dad.

If me and my sisters are heated with each other, this is *the* dis: "You act like *him*." Or "You look like *him* now with those scary eyes."

Once, Nikki said that and I stomped in front of the TV, huffing angry.

"Boy, if you don't move," Jess said.

Nikki threw a pillow at me. "Move!"

"Why you say I look like *him*?"

My sisters' stares'll put holes through you. How Cyclops from *X-Men* would. That's how they eyed me.

But. I. Am. Not. My. stepdad.

CHAPTER 12

MY mom's face in the photo stuck in the frame of my mirror—*so soft*. I trace my fingers over her smile—*so gentle*.

Ma's an angel, for real. Love and pureness in her eyes.

How come no one says I'm like her? I wonder.

"What you doing?" Ma pokes her head in my door. Smile even softer in real life.

I never could figure it out. She's seen so much bad, but she's still so good. Doesn't always jump to the worst. Sees the best in people. Even after . . . him.

Ma's the only person in our projects I heard say, "Be a rainbow in someone's cloud."

She tells a lot of people that Maya Angelou quote.

Right now, she walks in with two things in her hands. A fourth-grade drawing of mine and some tape. "I want to hang this on your wall."

I watch her put it up.

"Why'd you stop drawing?"

I shrug. Back then my baby-soft hands were always sketching something.

"Maybe you could take it up again. You were so good."
She smiles as beautiful as a rainbow. "I see you in the hall
with Cole, encouraging him."

"He's a good kid."

"And you're a good influence on him, Trev. He really
looks up to you."

She turns to my wall and looks at my boxing posters.
"I remember when this wall was covered with the superheroes you drew."

I nod at my posters. "But these guys can fight in real
life. They're superheroes too."

She comes and soft-pinches my chin. "True. And
you're a real-life superhero. Not just because your body
is strong."

When she leaves to cook dinner, I stare at my fourth-
grade drawing, feeling mad cloudy, mad torn.

CHAPTER 13

THE knock on my door makes me think Ma's back.

But it's Jess.

She may be my stepsister, but she feels like blood. Her expressions match Ma's 100 percent, and the two of them can even finish each other's sentences.

Jess smiles at the drawing Ma taped up. "Nice to see your art. Can I sit?"

I like how she's so respectful. "Yeah. Go 'head. Ma put that up. She be finding my old drawings out the blue."

"Trev, you still have more?"

"Yep." I point at a sneaker box in my closet. "Joints are in there from so far back I can't remember."

"Can I see them?"

I go pull the box down and hand it to her.

She flips through drawings, naming heroes she knows. "Batman. Superman. Wonder Woman. Spider-Man. X-Men. Teen Titans." Then she holds one up. "Who is this? *This* is soooo good, Trev."

I stand next to her to see because it's been a while since I seen what she's eyeing. It's a drawing of someone I wish I was as strong as—The Rock, Dwayne Johnson. It's him in that *Black Adam* movie. "He has Shazam's powers."

She traces her finger over his face. I thought Jess would focus on his muscles because I really detailed his arms and chest, but she's zoned in on his face. "I'm trying to teach the kids at the community center how to shade a character's face like this," she says. "You're so good at showing emotions."

"Want me to show you how I did it? I might remember."

"No. I mean, yes. Maybe you could even come to my after-school program someday. Lots of kids are trying to draw better. You could help me teach art."

Is she for real? She really thinks I'm that nice with my hands that I can teach art? "But I haven't drawn for years. Don't know if I can. Or even want to anymore."

She picks up one of my hands and rubs her thumb over my cracked knuckles. "Trev. You should keep drawing. You're good. Promise you'll at least think about it."

Our eyes lock.

She's for-real asking and I can't *not* answer. She's my sister. "I promise."

CHAPTER 14

ME and P have seen lots of neighborhood fights. Some happened before P lived in my building, when we didn't know each other yet, but we were in the same crowd, watching. We retell them a lot. Like now.

Walking to the stadium, P asks, "'Member when your uncle Puff fought Whiz?" Then P adds, "Puff really your uncle?"

Nah, but that not P's business. "Yeah."

Puff and Whiz were about twenty. Giants to us. They stood in a small, square parking lot the size of a boxing ring. Puff's crew on his side; Whiz's on his.

They stepped face-to-face, respectful. Everyone heard Puff: "No one jumps in. After this, our beef is deaded."

Just like that, they high-fived, boxed.

Seeing that fight was when I first decided I had to learn how to throw hands. But I didn't know who'd teach me. Right now, I remember how I went home and spoke with Ma.

"I want to know how to box."

She smiled a smile that said, *It's funny you say that.* "Trev, your grandpa—my father—was so good at boxing he almost went pro."

My eyes probably almost popped out my head. "For real?"

"He sparred with famous people." She named names I didn't know.

"So fighting is in my blood?"

"Maybe. But he did that because there wasn't a lot of other ways he could make money. You have promise—other talents, choices. I don't want to see my baby's face punched up."

Right now, P interrupts my flashback and blows my mind. "When your uncle Puff fought Whiz was when I first ever thought, 'I'ma learn to box like them.'"

"Whaaaat?" I can't hold it in. "Thought that then too."

We laugh a little at that coincidence.

P turns to me. "Have you been in a one-on-one fight?"

"No. You?"

"Nah. You think you could take a punch?"

"Maybe. You?"

P says, "Let's find out. The rec is free and has boxing. Let's learn for real."

And that's how we first go in the rec.

CHAPTER 15

THE boxing gym in the rec stinks so smelly-socks bad, I nearly gag.

But just like in my projects, it's full of guys of all ages who eye other guys their same age like they hungry and other dudes their size are food. Everyone inspecting each other. I usually don't get stared down because my stepdad and his friends have a no-joke reputation and heads don't wanna war with them, so they don't start with me. In this gym, though, everyone slows their workouts to check out me and P. They have stares like the guys who jumped me.

When nightmares wake me up, I do push-ups and shadowbox. I look in the mirror and see it: A fire is in me. *I'm on fire.* In this gym, everyone has that fire—it's in their eyes, it's in them. We all on fire in here.

Anyplace lit with action has music. Parties, amusement parks, wherevs. Beats so loud they shake everything. Beats you feel that pump you up like blood in your veins. This boxing gym bumps hot beats. Right now, I don't know the rapper who's on, who barks and growls, *"Stop, drop—"*

Older heads know and rap along: *"Shut 'em down /
Open up shop . . ."*

Me and P walk, bop, and nod along. Soon the rapper
raps something I feel: *"All I know is pain / All I feel is rain . . ."*

Guys shadowbox, punch bags, and spar in the ring,
and this feeling runs through me: *These guys'll teach me
how to handle my stepdad.*

P taps me. "Walk harder. We look soft."

"Soft?"

He points at a guy and we imitate how he walks, but it
feels exaggerated.

I whisper, "I feel goofy."

He shakes his head. "Nah. You look tough. I wouldn't
mess with you. What about me?"

"Walk more like Killmonger in *Black Panther.*"

P tries. "Better?"

"If Killmonger is a panther, you someone's kitten. Bop
harder."

He does.

We go through this gym and play close to walls so
we don't step in no one's way. We eye heads how they
eye us.

One by one, everyone sees we not soft and goes back
to working out.

Boxing bags explode and sway. Dudes loud-count their
sit-ups, pull-ups. Jump ropes blur invisible fast. Grunts
everywhere.

"P, being here is right."

"Why?"

"Because after this, we ready for whatever."

"Word," he agrees. "For any kid wanting beef, right?"

That's not who I mean.

CHAPTER 16

HEADS in this gym remind me of family. But these guys here are alive and around. Guys in my family are locked up, dead, ghost somewhere. I think of how Grandpa on Ma's side would fit in here because he boxed. Wish I met him. I bet he would've knocked my stepdad out.

Me and P stand to the side and watch. Each trainer eyes us like maybe they want me and P to come say hi. Every trainer except one. I'm curious why he's not curious.

And what's up with his cowboy strut? Dude walks like he just rode a horse for hours. Leans on one leg, then swings the other to step forward.

I tap P. "Bust his sheriff walk. You think his bop is real or fake?"

P shrugs.

We keep looking.

Another trainer jabs at a guy he's training and dude ducks down, comes up, and throws some air punches. The trainer isn't happy and it shows in his angry claps. "No! No! No!"

Me and P's eyes go back to the trainer with the cowboy walk. Same kind of thing happens there—he jabs at the guy he's training and dude ducks, then comes up with a flurry of air punches. But this trainer responds by throwing his arms open wide with love. "My man! I couldn't have done it better at your age. Next time, though, try this trick. Twist-snap your punches like a whip. Like this. Whip it, *pap! pap!*"

I elbow P. "You see how he's different?"

P nods. "He's mad chill."

We stand there a few more seconds, peeping how he treats another guy he's training. Homeboy's Tom Holland–Spider-Man fit and he does this jump-rope routine from *Creed.* Just as he's jumping so fast his rope whistles that wind sound over and over, the cowboy trainer limps to him. "Easy, easy. Save your legs. You sparring later and that's where your power comes from—your legs, your base. Take it easy, okay?"

It's hard to stop staring at this cowboy trainer. It's cool how he keeps the vibe calm and how he cares—like a good dad would.

CHAPTER 17

FOR two straight weeks me and P hit the rec every morning before school and find a spot to work out in.

Once, me and P overhear two guys.

"Do it how Cassius Clay would," the one with the gold front tooth says.

"Who?" the guy with no shirt on asks.

"The GOAT, Muhammad Ali. That's Cassius Clay."

Maybe I can't stop watching them because they're both built like the Hulk.

They start doing knuckle push-ups.

One Hulk grunts, "Ali said when it hurts, *then* start counting."

Me and P see them try that. It's bananas. They pass twenty. Then thirty. After fifty, I lose count.

When they stop, I tap P. "How many they just did?"

"Like seventy each?"

"Let's do like them. Like Ali. Count after our muscles start hurting."

P eyes me funny. "For real?"

"Yeah. Me first."

"Nah," P says, "let's do them together."

So we get in push-up position. We go down at the same time. Up at the same time.

At maybe fifteen, P huffs, "Y'feel it?"

I grunt, "Starting to."

He groans, "Me too."

I moan, "Okay, count NOW."

So we huff-count. "One . . . two." On the sixth, maybe seventh, our arms shake. At twelve or thirteen, our bodies shake. When P farts, our chests hit the floor and we bust out laughing, for just a second. Because heads here don't smile.

I hide my smirk. "Bruh, you *farted*."

P sucks his teeth. "Because that was the *hardest*."

"Facts." The hardest, funnest thing we did here.

CHAPTER 18

EXERCISING so early messes up my energy, and my tired shows in school. Right now, it's English class with Ms. Clark. She's a mom with two kids. One son's my age and she told me he looks like me. Makes sense since she looks like Ma. Same light brown skin and same hairstyle, pulled back and up in a bun. Just different heights. Ma's a shorty. Not Ms. Clark. She's not tall-tall. Just tall. She's not from my projects. Not from any hood. She's told us stories of her parents: "College sweethearts. Like their parents." So she ain't from here but her heart's here. She's one of our ride-or-die teachers. Goes to bat for any of us. Thinks of us.

She starts her Dr. King lesson with "An eye for an eye leaves everybody blind."

All my exercising hits me. My messed-up sleep from nightmares hits me. Lately, it happens here prolly because Ms. Clark is late in the day?

She asks us, "Why do you think King said that?"

Some kids raise hands.

I stand my textbook up so she thinks I'm reading. I wonder, *How tall is this book?* I rest my chin in my hand. *Boom.* I must have fallen asleep because next thing I know class is empty and Ms. Clark is talking to me.

"Trevor?"

"Yes, Ms. Clark?" I get my head up off the desk.

"Are you okay?"

I nod. "Just sleepy. Sorry."

"You been sleepy a lot. What grade did you get on your last report card in my class?"

"Eighty-five."

"Do you think you're earning that in this marking period?"

I shrug.

"Not with you sleeping in class."

"I'm sorry, Ms. Clark," I say. "King is cool but not what I need for real life right now."

"Why not?"

So much I want to say but it's too personal. I can't go in-in. "Stuff going on at home. My stepdad's gone."

Saying that felt awkward. Now Ms. Clark stares me dead in my eye. "Is there anything I can do to help?"

I shake my head.

She cocks her head at me. "Really?"

"I'm cool. I'm good for now."

She keeps on. "If you don't want to talk to me, there are other school adults who can help you."

I stand. "Ms. Clark, I gotta go." At the door, I feel grimy because she's dope and she was just being nice. "I'm sorry."

"I'm sorry too. You have promise. I'd hate for you to waste it."

That word again. *Promise.*

CHAPTER 19

THE train home is packed. Adults. Kids. Black, White, Latino, Asian, everything. Charter school kids in uniforms. Kids in regular gear like me. Crowd's kinda thick, but I feel alone. I bet these smiley kids don't have a stepdad about to get out of jail.

Kids about fourth-grade age chat next to me. One spins a fidget spinner.

Dang, I think, *haven't seen one of them in a minute.*

It spins so fast but stays in one spot.

I've felt that way since my stepdad got locked up two years ago. Life kept moving, spinning. At twelve, I'm much bigger than I was at ten—almost as big as my stepdad. Muscly. Feel stronger, but not. Feel ready, but not. And sometimes I still feel ten, in a bad way. All this hate. This fear. It's been holding on to me. Holding me in place. I feel like I got locked up when my stepdad did. His being stuck has me stuck. His promise to Ma has me stuck.

Parents with a son about my age catch my eye, and

the father smiles. The dad laughs with his son, strokes
his wife's arm. Bet he keeps sweet promises to her. Son's
so innocent-looking. Like he can be a kid. Life not heavy
like mine.

Don't have to keep promises like mine.

Ms. Clark told me, "You have promise."

Nah. This family here has promise. Their son is free.
Not stuck. He has a different promise. I eye the other kid's
fidget spinner. Spins so fast, stuck in one place. Stuck. In.
One. Place.

CHAPTER 20

TWO weeks at the rec becomes three. It's the same old, same old. Just me and P sticking together. Even how we exercise is the same.

I ask, "Why we here if we ain't switch it up?"

"How?"

I point at the ring. "There—" That's when I spot that cowboy-walking trainer staring real curious at me.

"P, is old dude with the cowboy bop eyeing us?"

"Nah, Trev, he's eyeing you."

And he does. Squints at me now and then like he's placing my face. Except he don't know me. We never met.

But I *want* to meet him.

I tap P. "Let's go see why he's staring."

CHAPTER 21

FRIENDS are friends with their crew. Let someone new approach them, and they shut down how stores close. You roll up; they stop talking. Eyes go from life's sweet to you stink. It happens now as me and P approach.

The cowboy trainer's boys snarl at us, trying to make us U-turn.

P's eyes are shook.

"Don't back out." I elbow him.

P swallows hard. "Doing this for you."

The cowboy trainer spots us and motions dudes he's training to get back to working out. Then he smiles at me. "'Sup?"

Don't be too thirsty.

Don't be soft.

I point at the ring. "We want to train with you."

I can feel P eye me like *WHAT? WE?! We do?*

CHAPTER 22

ME and P have always been good at guessing things. Especially names. Heads' nicknames match their styles. A bit after we became cool, we figured some out.

"Ace," P guessed, "for his handball serves."

"Whiz," I bet, "for his b-ball speed."

"Tuff don't smile." P nodded. "And Puff sells."

"No he don't," I said, lying to protect Uncle Puff. But everyone *knows*—Puff sells.

I bet P has cowboy names figured out for this trainer, but the trainer surprises us both when he says, "I'm Quick."

"*Quick*"? *How he quick when he walks so slow, rocking side to side?*

He asks us our names, ages, grades.

As we answer, he only studies my face—with a look that says *I know you–know you.*

When we stop speaking, he points at me. "You had an uncle named Lou?"

Wow. Quick is good at guessing things too.

This the second time he throws me off.

"Yeah. Lou was my uncle."

"Lou told me about you."

"About me? *Me*-me?"

"You Trev, ain't you?"

"Yeah."

"Your uncle Lou was family to me."

CHAPTER 23

FAMILY.

Blood-related men in my family are sun before night. They here, shining for a bit. Then gone. Leaving things dark and my head be in the clouds. Searching for sun. Wish I had sun but get none. Sometimes feels like I never had sun.

My uncles are more family. Well, they not my blood uncles. Like Uncle Puff. He's not blood. But he acts like family. So they family.

My uncles are trees in my projects. Concrete hardness everywhere, building after building and block after block. But a tree pops up every now and then, reminding me of what's different. That all this hardness ain't normal. That it ain't normal to be without sun.

You know, the sun helps trees grow.

Men in my fam helped raise my uncles. It's why these uncles help raise me. They're why I know about blood-related men in my fam. My uncles tell me about them so I don't feel 100 percent without sun.

CHAPTER 24

UNCLE Lou was Ma's brother, my blood uncle who she says I look like. He died when I was four. Ma says I was his heart. Says I clung to him like he was my heart too. I don't remember him. Wish I did.

Most people say I'm like my stepdad, not knowing we not blood. So I don't expect it when Quick says, "Boy, Trev, you your uncle Lou's *twin*." On the outside, I hide how I feel. But I love it. *Uncle Lou's twin.* I love someone sees I'm not my stepdad.

Ma also called Uncle Lou a gentle giant. Gentlest guy unless you burned him. In a gang, but shouldn'ta been. Hard because he had to be. Did what he had to but shouldn't've.

Ma keeps his photo in her bedroom mirror. Uncle Lou flashes a wide, kiddie smile. Men around here don't usually smile so free that way. They'd get called soft. Being soft's not good here. Mostly everyone, everything, is stone. But soft is Lou, just like hard was too.

"This photo," Ma once said, "is how he could've been if things were different."

CHAPTER 25

QUICK is talking to me but I'm focused on his forearm tat—it's Uncle Lou's tat.

"You listenin', kid?" Quick snaps me back to hearing.

P is thirsty. "Who's Lou?"

I want to say, P, *this is an A and B conversation. C your way out.* So I'm glad when Quick asks P, "Can you go hit that bag for three minutes, show me what you got?"

P leaves to hit the bag.

"Man, Trev. It's really you. How's your moms? She was his heart. Man, you take after Lou so much."

I nod. "Ma's good."

"So . . . why you here?"

I lift my fist. "Tryna be nice with my hands."

"Why? Someone messin' with you?"

"Nah. Just need to know how to fight."

"Because?"

"It's wild out here."

"I know. I used to live here."

"You don't anymore?"

"Nah. My wife wanted to move. So I come here, train, go home. Get out."

Out—how he says it sounds nice.

"So tell me," Quick says, "why you want to fight?"

"Mainly to protect my mom and sisters."

"You know what'll help them more? Graduate high school. Go to college. Help them move out of here. Somewhere safe. That was Lou's dream for you." Quick waves at boxers boxing. "This ain't Lou's dream for you."

"How you a trainer but say fighting is bad?"

"I'm not saying fighting is bad. It's just that I remember you in your uncle's arms. He'd show you off. He made a bunch of us huddle and promise. 'This *our* nephew, y'hear? And if you ever see him be like me, stop him. Make sure Trev sticks with school. Tell him not to think with fists. *Promise.*' We promised."

Promise—there's that word again. I remember my promise. The one I made after my stepdad made his from the cop car. So I tell Quick, "I need to know how to fight. You train kids? Train me."

"No."

"Then I'll go ask another trainer—"

"No you won't. No one'll train you in this gym."

"Why not?"

"Because I'm telling them not to."

"But I do good in school. How's this? If I do *real-real* good and show you my grades, you train me? My uncle

Lou'd want me to protect my family." I lift up my fists. "With these."

"No, he'd want you to be different."

I'm so pissed he has me here begging and I can't think of anything else to say to convince him. "A'ight." I give up and walk off.

"Wait, youngblood," Quick says. "See you soon?"

"Nah. You said don't come here."

"I didn't say that. I *said* me and my guys won't train you. Come back, though. To kick it."

The look in his eyes is the same as my stepdad's friends': He wants to keep an eye on me, help me. But he can't help me all the way if he can't teach me to throw hands.

"Sure," I say, but I feel, *Nah.*

CHAPTER 26

I go find P. "Let's go. We out."

"Why?"

"C'mon." Outside I tell P, "Forget the rec."

"Why?"

"No one'll train us."

"How come?"

"Because Quick won't let them."

"Why not?"

"Because he's wack. That's why." Then I tell P just enough about Uncle Lou. Feels good too, even though Ma says don't share family business.

"Sorry your uncle got killed," P tells me.

I don't know what to say. "I'ma take a walk. By myself."

P looks at me a long time. "I get it. I got you."

P goes his way, me mine.

As I walk, I got Uncle Lou in my head. His words, what he told Quick. Wish Lou had been here to handle my stepdad. Wish he was here now so we could talk.

Other not-blood uncles pop up in my mind. Ones I can talk to. Maybe I should visit one now.

Then another thought pops into my head. *Quick and Uncle Lou's tat. Who else has that tat?*

My mind starts picturing uncles until I say, "Uncle Frankie."

CHAPTER 27

I jet through my stepdad's corner. Men nod and fist-bump me and pat me on the back, but since I'm not here to see them, I keep walking.

Straight.

To.

That.

Garage.

Right.

There.

Uncle Frankie's garage.

I cross the street, and as soon as I hit the curb, it smells of oil and gas. Might smell bad to some. Smells mad good to me.

Out front there's a parking lot full of broke-down cars. Some stacked on each other how two slices of bread be. I do what I used to before going in to see Frankie. I go sit in a busted car.

"*Mm-mm,*" I hum as my hands grip the steering wheel and my mind time-travels to when I used to come here all the time when I was little because my day care was next door. Every afternoon I'd play here until Ma or my real dad came after their jobs.

Right now I remember back to when I was Little Cole's age and I'd be here behind the wheel imagining me chasing or escaping bad guys.

CHAPTER 28

REAL quick, Uncle Frankie's face pops up in the window, smiling big how he does every time he sees me. "Trev, you speed-racing again?"

"Yeah." I get out of the car. "Uncle, can we *talk*-talk?"

"C'mon." He jerks his head, and as I follow, his huge, wide, muscly back reminds me of what all my friends who see him say: "Your uncle looks like The Rock."

"Dwayne Johnson?" Uncle Frankie once joked when he overheard my homeboy Ethan say that. "But does The Rock have this haircut?" Uncle palmed his head.

We both laughed. "Yes he does!!!" because they have the same bald-shaven haircut.

"Okay," he kept on, "but does The Rock have this?" Then he body-build-curled his arm. Yo, his bicep was bigger than a grapefruit and his forearm was thicker than a half gallon of milk.

"Yes!" Ethan shouted.

Uncle kept joking with him. "But he can't do this," and he raised one eyebrow.

Ethan and I cracked up. "Yes he can!" he said. "That's The Rock's eyebrow move."

I liked Ethan. Too bad he moved away.

Anyway, that time with Ethan reminded me of how funny Uncle Frankie can be and how much this garage used to be my spot.

It was my uncle Lou who got him his job here at the garage. Uncle Frankie started sweeping here. Now he's a manager.

He once told me, "Your uncle Lou's a lifesaver. He helped me leave the gang. I was just a kid when I joined, and Lou told me rolling with them might get me killed. Our gang? You got beat up to join and beat up to leave. But Lou protected me. Didn't let me get stomped on to get out. But he did warn me: 'I promise, I'll beat you if you ever rejoin.'"

Feels how Lou was with Frankie is how Frankie is with me. He keeps me on the right path and away from what could get me hurt.

This garage saved Frankie, and in a way, this garage saved me too.

Always felt safe here. Loved. I feel that now as Uncle waves me into his office. Plants all over. I joke, "Like Jurassic Park in here. Expecting a T. rex to pop up."

He chuckles and starts snapping dead leaves off a plant. I go sit on his couch that's an old back seat of a car. It's got coils sticking out that can rip your pants, but still, I love this car seat–couch.

Above it, there's a napkin taped to the wall in Uncle's handwriting. *Be a rainbow in someone's cloud.*

I guess he likes that quote from Ma too.

"Soda?" Uncle Frankie now hands me one.

"No doubt." I take it and pop it open.

In my heart, I'm that little day care boy again, feeling freer.

CHAPTER 29

FAMILY knows you. Can tell if something's up from just eyeing you. They spot what's different.

"'Sup with your red knuckles?" Uncle Frankie points.

I stuff my fists in my hoodie's pocket.

He plays along. "Okay, so what we talkin' about?"

I jump into it. "You know Quick?"

On instinct, his eyelid stress-twitches and one hand touches his forearm tat. His reaction says more than he says. "Yeah. How you know Quick?"

I lift my cracked knuckles in a fighter's pose. "Met him today at the rec. He trains boxers there."

Uncle Frankie leans forward and his mood flips. "He training you?!" He's so heated I want to lie to see what he says if I say yeah. But he's real with me. Gotta be real with him.

"Nah. Says he promised Uncle Lou he wouldn't. So, how y'all know each other?"

He relaxes, glad from what I said. "Yeah. Brothers for life. Meet once in a blue."

"Cool. Then do me a solid? Tell him to train me?"

"Nah. He's right. Lou didn't want you fighting. You gotta be different."

There that goes again: *different*. Now I know I'm in the right spot for answers. "Why'd Uncle Lou say that?"

"You ever see a grown man be a boy? A tough guy be soft as cotton balls? You was born and Lou got that way. Proud-parent-like. He'd be in our spot with your baby photo. Acting like you was his son. His second chance. You know, he was street, but not street. We were in the gang to give our families protection, money. But Lou always said he wanted different—especially once you were born."

I want to say so much, but these words fly out. "But I need to fight because of my stepdad. He hit my mom."

The way Frankie falls back in his seat, you'd think I blasted him.

"That's messed up," he says.

Then straight trash comes out of his mouth. "But it's for them to deal with. It's your parents' business."

Whoa. What? I know Uncle Frankie loves Ma. Is he saying this since he's my stepdad's boy too? He can't be scared of him, because Uncle Frankie is way bigger.

I'm so mad I want to make him mad too. "My fists are this way from boxing."

"But you said Quick don't train you."

"He doesn't. But I've been practicing since my stepdad

went away. He threatened Ma for calling the cops. If he's out, he'll hurt her. And I'm bodying him."

"You can't do that, Trev."

"Because why? Because Uncle Lou wouldn't want me to?"

"Cuz, Trev, you hurtin' your stepdad leads to things. And that'll kill your mother. That'll kill me too. It'll kill all of us."

I ask, "Lead to what things?"

He shrugs. "Stuff. You involved with cops."

"But, Uncle Frankie," I say it how P did, "sometimes you just gotta throw hands."

"You ever *had* to use these"—he lifts his gigantic fists and stares sad at them—"on someone? It's not what you think."

There's so much I want to shout. Like:

What I think about having to throw hands don't matter!

My stepdad doesn't think twice before throwing hands!

I don't want him coming back!

Uncle Frankie, help!

I'm so angry at my uncle for saying this is my parents' business. I slit my eyes at him, thinking, *How can you not care about what me, Ma, and my sisters are going through?*

I open my mouth to speak but think again. "Forget it." I pull out my cell. "Got a text. Gotta bounce."

"Really?" Hustlers know when you hustle them. Uncle Frankie nods at my cell. "So, who texted?"

I put my phone away so he can't see no one did, and I head to the door.

"Hold up, Trev. I want you to understand where I'm coming from—"

"Nah, we good." I fake a smile. "I'll catch you later."

He knows I'm thinking there's no "later." But I leave before he can say more.

CHAPTER 30

OUTSIDE, Frankie's words are in my head: *You hurtin'*
your stepdad . . . it'll kill all of us. How's he gonna say "all of
us"? Wish I had asked him, "How's there an 'us'? What 'us'
stopped my stepdad from hurting Ma? No one. You know
why? Because there's no 'us.'"

Also should've asked, "And, Frankie, who'll stop my
stepdad next time? Not you. You said it's not your business. So, *boom*, no 'us' again."

It's all on me.

It hurts because I thought Frankie would always be
"us."

I'm already too tight by the time I pass my school.
Then a banner over the door says: IT TAKES A VILLAGE
TO RAISE A CHILD. I hear Frankie's "us" again in my head
and suck my teeth. These thoughts explode in me: *Even*
school lies. Saying we have a village. There is no "us," "we," or
"village."

If there was, someone would've stopped my
stepdad—or would help now.

CHAPTER 31

AS I get close to my stepdad's corner, other uncles smile, nod, wave at me. *Ugh. Probably more fake-village.* I'd avoid this corner if I could.

Uncle Puff's there and heads for me. The Puff who fought Whiz. At least Puff's not my stepdad's boy. He's Ma's homeboy since they were little.

Uncle Puff's diesel arm pythons my neck. He's almost as muscly as Uncle Frankie, so it's hard to wriggle free of his hold. Usually, I don't want to. Right now, I do because I'm still in my feelings from Frankie's garage. Uncle Puff's street ESP is as strong as Spider-Man's Spider-Sense. He lets me go and shakes me. "Why you sour?"

My stepdad's friends are watching. I guess I eye them funny. Uncle Puff catches that too and U-turns me away from this corner.

Soon, we near his car. It's as dip as rappers on social media. One look and you know it costs money. When he drives, his rims spin in a hypnotizing way.

Uncle Puff taps his key to unlock it. "You hungry?"

I nod.

"So get in. Let's go eat and grab food for your moms and sisters."

I get in his car and watch Uncle Puff's diamond-ringed hand steer the wheel.

Admiring his ice makes me think less about Uncle Frankie. "How much your right-hand ring cost?"

He huffs. "This? This is nothing. Now, your grades. That's something. You still get eighty-fives and up?"

I stare out the window. "Yeah. Mostly."

"Lucky. I was a fifties, sixties, barely passing kid. Would've been fly to have your brains. I'd be Jay-Z now. Making billions."

"You doing a'ight," I say, looking around his leather-interior car and gear.

I remember asking Ma about him. "How Uncle Puff wears the best?"

She sighed. "Because Uncle Puff does the worst. Still, you not God. Don't judge him."

Ma is that way. She knows a lot but isn't a know-it-all judgy type.

CHAPTER 32

UNCLE Puff drives us to a hero shop on the edge of our projects. Every kind of customer here. Cops. Hustlers. Lawyers. Construction workers. More. White, Black, Latino, Asian, whatevs.

A teacher once said in some countries wars aren't allowed. That's this shop—it's a safe spot. Uncle Puff's brought me here before. Heads order heroes, mind their biz. Workers treat customers like we big and call us "chief," "big man" . . .

One tells me now, "Hey, boss, you ready?"

Boss. That sounds nice. Maybe because I don't feel boss a lot.

Uncle Puff elbows me. "Get anything."

I order my favorite: "Salami, cheese, lettuce, tomato, mayonnaise, on the softest Italian roll."

The worker nods at Puff. "And you, captain? What you wanna make happen?"

Uncle Puff palms my head. "Make mine the same as my nephew's."

"That's it? Two heroes?"

"Nah," Uncle Puff tells him, then me, "Order food to bring home to your moms and sisters."

"Ma would want pastrami and melted mozzarella."

The counter guy shouts that to someone making our heroes.

I try to remember what Jess and Nikki like. Yo, the last time I messed up Jess's hero order, she reminded me, "Me and Nikki always get the same thing. Roast turkey, ham, tomato, and cheddar. And a bag of those sour-cream-and-onion potato chips. Pork rinds for Ma."

I order that.

Uncle Puff elbows me. "Cool. If your stepdad was out, what would he want?"

"Forget him."

Puff nods like he solved a riddle. "Mmm-mm. Yeah. You sour because of *him*."

CHAPTER 33

"THAT'S your spot," Uncle Puff says as he cruises his car by the stadium.

"How you know?"

He chuckles. "Maybe my people drive by and see? Maybe I do? So why you box out there?"

I pump a fist. "Tryna get my hand skills like yours. Remember when you bodied Whiz?"

"Someone messing with you?"

I stay quiet, thinking.

He keeps on. "If yeah, I'll handle it. Who is it?"

Okay, I think, *Uncle Puff isn't Uncle Frankie. He wants to get involved.*

"Speak, Trev."

I want to tell him about my stepdad. Get Uncle Puff to make him stop. But what if Uncle goes too far? Do I want my stepdad to end up . . . ?

"Cool. Don't say. I'll find out."

"How?"

"Your moms."

Puff *can't* ask Ma.

"Nah," I say, "don't let her know. You handled Whiz solo. Let me do me."

"So, someone *is* messing with you."

"Nah. Just a punk. A bully. We'll shoot a fair one. It'll be done."

We stop at a red light and Uncle Puff looks at me. "You know I got you, right?"

"For sure. Yeah."

"And only cuz you ask, I'll stay out of it. But if you need—"

"Thanks, Uncle Puff. That's all I need. Just be here for me. Like now."

CHAPTER 34

NIKKI and Jess come in together while I'm in the kitchen doing homework.

Like usual, Nikki hits the fridge first. So she sees first. "Where'd heroes come from?"

I say, "I got them with Uncle Puff."

Then I jump up and move quick—imagining I have the Flash's Speed Force. I grab plates and napkins from the cupboard and set the table.

Jess elbows Nikki and smiles proudly at my hustle.

"You want help?" Jess asks.

She's oldest and sometimes Nikki copycats her. Like now. "Yeah. You want help?"

"Nah. Sit. Be comfortable."

Jess winks at Nikki, then tells me, "That's nice of you."

They watch me unwrap the heroes. "There's potato chips too."

Ma comes out and nods, real impressed at what I'm doing.

I clap my hands. "Done. Come sit."

They do, and sometime while eating, I realize I'm watching them more than I eat. *They look so happy. Nobody's talking because they're enjoying their heroes.*

Then all of a sudden, I taste it. I check. "They forgot my tomatoes."

"It's okay," Nikki says. She lifts the bread off the untouched half of her hero and plucks tomatoes from it for me. "Here, Trev. I have a lot."

I'm surprised, but I don't tell her she doesn't have to be so nice to me. Usually Nikki's arguing with me. But this dinner has us getting along and loving each other—and I like it.

"This was nice of Puff," Ma says. "I'm going to knit him a scarf. I have a bunch of yarn left over. Don't tell him. It'll be a surprise."

I sit here, feeling what I think we all feel tonight: taken care of. Me and Uncle Puff did this, and it's dip.

I want us to feel this vibe all the time.

CHAPTER 35

I'M up early and still feel good about last night and taking care of my family. Now I want to take care of them again. The thought hits me, *Make them breakfast.*

I try to remember what they eat. "Jess eats . . ." I pour her cornflakes. "Nikki . . ." I make toast. "Ma . . ." I scramble eggs. *Everyone eats eggs. Make more.*

Dang, it be nice to make Ma's coffee. I grab the coffee can. *Nah, you'll mess it up, Trev.*

I move Superman fast before they up.

When Nikki comes out, she squints. "How's breakfast done when Ma's—?"

Jess is next out. "Breakfast is made?"

I nod, proud. "I did this. *I got you.*"

Nikki is tougher. "My toast better not be burnt."

Jess: "Ungrateful. For that, Trev, *burn* Nikki's toast."

Now Ma walks in. "Who made breakfast?"

"Trev," Nikki and Jess say together.

The look on Ma's face. She's a rainbow. So's Jess. But my sister Nikki is a cloud. Throwing me mad shade.

But Ma's and Jess's love shines right through.

CHAPTER 36

"HEY." Nikki pops her head into my room as I tighten my kicks' laces before going to school. She has that look of wanting to say something and I bet she's trying to word giving me props for breakfast. She does this sometimes— thanks me on the low.

I smile. "You liked my breakfa—"

"Pa sent Ma a letter."

All the air leaves me.

Nikki's eyes are upset. "Don't tell Ma I saw it. Don't say I told you. The letter was open on her dresser. Pa's definitely coming out this month."

My stomach flips. *Dang. Dang. Dang. Dang.*

"I thought you'd want to know."

"Yeah." I nod, feeling too many things to talk.

She shuts the door and comes and sits on the edge of my bed.

I try reading her face. "You good?" I ask.

She bites her lip. "You think he's the same? Better? Worse? What d'you think'll happen?"

I put my fist in my hand and stroke my red, cracked knuckles. "Like I know."

At the same time, we both inhale real deep, then exhale real hard.

She notices and smiles. "You copycatting me?"

I'm glad she's smiling because I want her to feel better, so I joke-soft-elbow her. "Puh-leez. *You* copying me."

"No, you tryna be me."

And we go back and forth, teasing and trying to forget how we really feel about our stepdad coming home.

CHAPTER 37

OUR fridge has mad magnets with places we never been. Friends visit and give them to Ma and keep us dreaming of places different from here.

Jess checks her makeup in one of the magnets that has a mirror. She sighs. "Ugh. I have a long day. School, then the community center."

"I'm going to see Rick later," Nikki says.

Maybe it's that Jess is older than Nikki or wants more for Nikki. Jess big-sisters her right now. "You still seeing Slicky Ricky? What? It's been a month already?"

Nikki gets tight. "Why you hatin'?"

"Maybe because he reminds me of a *con* artist. You put your *con*-fidence in him, and then find out he's fooled you."

"Why you beastin'?"

"I just want you to open your eyes, Nikki. Rick talks slick. Says what you want to hear. But can you trust him? I'm not sure he's all he says he is."

"How so?"

"Like he's always bragging about money, but you told me when you went to the movies you ended up paying for him. And he tries to pretend he's chill, but I always catch him peeking at your phone to see who you're talking to. To know who you're with."

"I like that he cares who I'm with," Nikki says.

"That's not caring—it's controlling. Soon, him being all in your business won't be cute," Jess warns Nikki. "Then what? And you're letting him get too comfortable in our apartment. Last time he spread out on the couch while you sat on the floor. Like he owns our place. And he knows he's not even supposed to be here when Ma's not."

Nikki leaves and slams her bedroom door.

I'm glad Jess said that about Rick. He's sus. If I had Spider-Sense, it'd be tingling "danger" every time he's around.

Don't let no one mess with your sisters. I think of the promise my stepdad made me make. But how can I protect Nikki when she doesn't protect herself?

Isn't blood thicker than who you dating? How come she always sides with her sus boyfriend, even when Jess is warning her? We family. We really care. Why do we always fight the wrong people? Flip on people who protect us. People who love us, we hit.

That's what my stepdad did. How come she didn't learn from that?

CHAPTER 38

WALKING home after school, I run into another uncle.

Uncle Larry isn't blood either, but he's always been family to us. Him and Ma been tight since they were in high school. If he's around, me and Ma stay laughing because he's funnier than most comedians.

Larry smiles big right now. "You going somewhere?"

He's a librarian in our projects' library and his whole apartment is books. Books on his couch. On shelves. Even his bathroom is a library.

And his comics collection is fire too. Some are classics—it's wild how different Batman's suit looked when Batman first came out and how the original Luke Cage wasn't bald but had a lollipop 'fro. I used to bring my drawings to him, and Uncle Larry loved them. "You know what I think? Keep this up and someday people here'll brag, 'Remember little Trev? Well, he's a famous comic book artist for a big studio who turns comics into movies.'"

"Uncle," I ask now as we walk, "what you reading lately?"

"Few books. You'd like them."

"You headed home? I can come see?"

"Sure," he says and dials my mom. "Hey, Bea, guess who I'm with. Yep, our future star illustrator. Can he come to my place?"

People who know Ma well call her Bea, short for Beatrice. She must be saying yes because he gives me a thumbs-up.

"You believe what you said?" I ask Uncle.

"What?"

"You really think I could really be an illustrator?"

"Yes! You just gotta stay on it. You got that talent, for sure, for sure."

We walk and he gets quizzy. "You know the value of things, right?"

"Maybe."

"Failing. Winning. What costs more?"

I shrug. "Dunno."

"It costs more if you fail."

"Okay. So stay winning?"

"What's 'winning'?"

"Winning is winning."

"Nah, explain. What's 'winning'?"

"Maybe it depends on who you are?"

"Right. It's in the eye of the beholder."

"The beholder?" I look at Uncle Larry's shining eyes. He's like Einstein and other geniuses. Whose treasure is in their heads. Like Puff's rings. Stuff Larry says is next level.

" 'It's in the eye of the beholder'—it's a quote I like."

"What's a beholder?"

He points at two middle school girls making a TikTok video. Then at other people out here. "Everyone is."

I laugh. "Because we all be holding?"

He chuckles. "Yes. You hold a lot. Your mind, your power."

The sun is blazing and the afternoon's getting hot, and I feel it again—my uncles are trees, and my six-foot-three Uncle Larry is one of the tallest, giving me good shade now, when I need it.

CHAPTER 39

UNCLE Larry's apartment is the same as always. Every tile on the floor could be a book because you can't walk without stepping on one. I love it.

We head to the kitchen and my eyes go to the fridge door—covered with pictures he's cut out of old photo magazines. "Where's President Obama and Jay-Z?" He has this fire photo of them at a party, laughing.

"I put it in a photo album."

I look back at his fridge. "Bruce Lee knew Jackie Chan?" They joke, on break from filming a movie.

"Oh yeah. Jackie was a kid then. Worshipped Bruce."

I sit down at his long table. One end is full of photos of Nipsey Hussle. Nips with Drake. Nips with Snoop Dogg. Nips with Ed Sheeran. Nips with Nick Cannon. Nips with DJ Khaled. Nips with James Harden. Nips with Odell Beckham.

"You doing a display on Nips for the library?" I ask.

"Good idea! I should. He showed what we can do, how to give back too."

Elbow to elbow, we stare at Nips. Nips is dead but feels alive here. "I think they all liked him for the same reason: what he represents. Promise. A rapper who gave his community hope. Started Black businesses. Tried ending gang violence. Showed there's another way."

"RIP, Nips, right?"

"Oh yeah. His loss is a loss for us all. Neighborhood Nips was in the middle. Coulda gone to any side. He chose helping. And he was winning until . . ." Uncle's eyes get sad-stormy.

I stare back at Nips and think of what Uncle Larry said: *What he represents. Promise . . .*

There's that word again.

Nips was in the middle. Coulda gone to any side. Am I in that same spot?

This thing with my stepdad has me in the middle, thinking where I might end up.

CHAPTER 40

WALKING back home, I let my feet move on auto. My body too.

A few fancy auto companies on the edge of our projects sell cars that drive on autopilot. Someone drove one on auto here, proving that moving on auto in my neighborhood is *bad*. The car hit a mom and daughter. Nah. Ran over them. They were under the bumper.

Right now, remembering that makes me inhale, exhale. *Get outta auto, Trev.* Quick, I realize where I'm at and where being on auto got me. I'm on one of the worst blocks.

But it's too late. Two troublemaker brothers my age, known for robbing kids, have spotted me. One yells, "Ayo, c'mere." They come off their stoop. "What you doin' around here?" They keep coming toward me.

I look around. Block's empty. Just us. I'm outnumbered. I don't move. They want me, they can come get me. I ball my fist and feel my red knuckles crack. These guys haven't seen me for a long time. They touch me? Watch what happens.

Just then a familiar voice spins me around.

"Trev, there you are!"

And here comes P running over.

I haven't been happier to see him.

These troublemaker brothers U-turn to their stoop.

Two-on-two is a fair fight.

They don't ever fight fair.

CHAPTER 41

LITTLE Cole is in the hall drawing when me and P step off the elevator.

"*Cole!*" we say at the same time, and I go kneel next to him. "Cole, your drawing's good enough to be in a comic book?"

"No," he sighs. "Sometimes drawing isn't so easy. Look. I think this corner needs something. Maybe a superhero who moves fast? What would you draw?"

"Someone fast?" P sits down crisscross-applesauce next to Cole, trying to help. "Maybe the Flash?"

"Nuh-uh." Cole puts his finger on a red blur. "I already have the Flash. See, right here?"

Me and P act like we could tell that's the Flash.

"Sure."

"Right."

"I need someone who *doesn't* have superspeed," Cole says. "A human who just fights fast."

I figure it's best to ask who he already drew. "Who else is in this drawing? Tell us and it'll help us see who's missing."

He names Marvel and DC characters we know.

P asks, "Cole, maybe me and Trevor can take turns calling out really quick human-type heroes until you hear who you want?"

Cole's face flips to excited. "Go ahead."

P goes first. "Captain America?"

Cole shakes his head.

I jump in. "Daredevil?"

He twists his lips no.

"Black Widow?"

He cocks his head, a maybe.

I tap my finger to my chin, thinking, then snap. "Catwoman?"

"No," he says.

Me and P say at the same time, "Black Panth—"

Cole ends what we're saying. "Panther! The Black Panther is missing." He grabs his colored pencil, and me and P smile at each other.

We watch him for a few seconds, then P asks, "You want us to stay?"

Cole's in another world, so zoned in. "No, thank you."

We go to my apartment, but at my door, I stare one last time at Cole. Naming heroes brought me back to when I was his age. When choosing which hero to draw was my biggest worry. Sorta wish I could go back to that time.

CHAPTER 42

"**MA?**" I open our apartment door.

No answer.

"Nikki?" Silence.

"Jess?"

YO-ooo! I smile. "No one's home."

P smiles back. "Dope."

Boom, now we got a nice chill escape.

I grab my OJ from the fridge and swig. *Mmm. Extra sweet.*

Maybe extra sweet from how swee-eeet it is to have the apartment to myself. "P, we have another container of juice. Want?"

"Yeah."

"Hit my room. I'll pour and bring yours."

P dips there, and the next thing I hear is P holler, "DANG!"

His shout almost makes me spill his OJ as I walk in my room. "Bruh, what?!"

"TREV! This drawing is *TIGHT*!"

Ugh. He scared me over the drawing Ma put on my wall?

"I didn't know you drew this good!"

"That's from way back when I was ten."

"Wow! Why'd you stop drawing?!"

I hear his question twice. First, how he asked it. Then Ma in my head when she asked the same thing.

Maybe it's seeing Little Cole in the hallway drawing and that vibe. I want that feeling right now. The feeling from sketching.

P maybe reads my mind. "Yo, let's draw now? I haven't in years neither."

I hand him his OJ. "My drawing skills is prolly trash."

"Mine prolly is doo-doo."

"A'ight." I go grab pens and paper.

Minutes of sketching pass. I'm curious. "What you drawing?"

"A lion." P shows me.

My stepdad's sign is Leo, a lion. "That lit, P. But why a lion?"

"Kings of the jungle. Not scared. Uncaged."

Keys jingling interrupts us.

I crack open my door and peek at the apartment door as it slowly opens.

Wait? What?! Nah!

CHAPTER 43

NIKKI walks in with her boyfriend, Rick, and his crew—even though she knows not to bring *guys* here. Ma's told her a hundred times: *No boyfriends if I'm not here.*

Rick purrs, fake kittenlike. "We alone?"

Nikki says, "Definitely."

Trap music blasts from a phone, killing the quiet, and Rick's guys start shouting.

I peek out my room again, and they're having a pillow fight. It reminds me of what Jess told Nikki about how Rick acts in our apartment. *Like he owns our place.* Like he can sit wherever he wants, do whatever he wants.

Ma's pillows, I think. She made those. *Why is Nikki letting them wild out?*

P peeks over my shoulder. "Bruh, they disrespecting your apartment. Your mom cool that they here?"

Maybe it's what P says? Maybe it's how he says it?

Maybe it's my anger. I swing open my door and step out.
"Nikki, *why* they here without Ma?"

Her eyes pop to the size of boiled eggs.

Rick sucks his teeth. "Oh, it's you."

Rick and his crew chuckle. Their eyes ask me, *What you gonna do?*

CHAPTER 44

NIKKI'S face is still straight shocked. "You home?"

Duh? Why she asking if it's obvi I'm home?

My words come out with mad force. Because they're not mine—I'm repeating Ma's words since I feel she'll respect Ma. "Ma says, no boyfriends if she ain't here."

"She does?" Her questioning me sounds so goofy. She *knows* Ma says that.

Rick steps in. "Trev, why you acting foul? Just go in your room. Let us be here."

"You can't."

"No?" he snarls, like he's not leaving.

"Nikki," I say. "Fine. Stay and I'll call Ma."

Her eyes pop even bigger and she eyes Rick. "We can't be here."

Rick and his boys glare at me. Them and Nikki head to the door. But their music stays loud. If I were Spider-Man, my Spider-Sense would be more than buzzing. This doesn't feel over.

Our apartment door slams. *BAM!*

They gone, then I remember, *Little Cole is in the hall.*
I rush out and check. Whew, he's gone. Good.

But Nikki and Rick and his guys seem real comfortable in our hall with their music turned up.

They not going anywhere.

It's not over.

CHAPTER 45

DON'T *let no one mess with your sisters.* I hear my step-dad's voice in my head.

P interrupts, "Back to try *drawing?*"

I stand in the middle of my living room, staring at our closed apartment door, and hear the hall music. I feel east and west. I came home for peace and quiet and don't want drama with Rick and them. But Nikki's in the hall.

"My sister with them don't feel right."

P shrugs. "I hear her laughing, so she's probably good."

I strain, listening harder for that. But then I hear Nikki shout, dead serious, "STOP!"

I jet into the hall.

Rick's all on her, gripping her arms.

She repeats, *"Stop."*

Rick's boys flip from zoned out to zoned in. They eye me how guys in the rec eyed us when we first showed up—eyeing like they hungry and we food. The stares of the guys who jumped me.

"Trev, who said come out here?"

"Go in your apartment."

"If your sister needs you, she'll say."

I yell past them at Rick. "Leggo Nikki."

They step toward me.

My stomach and legs start to tremble. They must smell I'm scared. They snarl-grin more. "Yeah. You know you want to bounce."

I feel caged. But Nikki's eyes are so scared-young, saying, *Don't leave me.*

"Nikki, come in with us."

Rick squeezes her arm. "Stay."

"Ouch!" She tries pulling away.

Rick tells me, "Just bounce, Trev," and something in me explodes.

This is *my* sister!

This is *my* building!

Rick is the one who better bounce.

CHAPTER 46

RICK lets go of Nikki and puts his fists up in fighter pose. He throws a punch at my face. I don't flinch and his fist stops an inch from my nose.

Rick soft-pushes me. "Punk."

I shove Rick to the side, go to the window, and—*punch!* CRAAAAAASH!!! My fist goes right through it.

Glass tinks all over the floor.

These windows are thick. Never saw one fully break. I just broke it.

The hall gets mad quiet.

Rick's crew's mouths hang open like they can't believe it.

"What Trev hit that with?"

"Rick . . . that almost was your face."

I U-turn to Rick. Life slo-mos. I feel . . . uncaged.

His snarl melts.

Then Nikki speaks: "Trev. Your. *Hand.*"

"Huh?" It's like she wakes me up.

"You bleeding!"

Everything speeds up. I look at my fist.

Drip . . .

Drip . . .

Drip.

Red dots keep hitting the floor—blood leaking from my knuckles. *Drip-drip-drip . . .*

Then I see *him.*

Little Cole.

Eight years old.

Standing at his apartment door.

Trying to make sense of what he's seeing.

His face says a lot without words. He's scared, confused. This isn't the hall he's used to. This isn't the me he's used to.

Cole turns to head back inside.

I open my mouth to speak, then I hear it. A police walkie-talkie outside. I rush-peek out the window.

A cop points at us. "Stay up there! Do NOT move!"

CHAPTER 47

"**THE** cops!" Rick and his crew don't waste any time. They fly upstairs to our roof, where they'll hop on another roof and exit down its stairwell onto a block where cops aren't waiting.

Nikki tells P, "Bring my brother inside, quick!"

"Huh?" P is as clueless as me.

"Cops'll arrest Trev for the window."

"Oh, dip!" P shoves me toward my door. "C'mon, Trev!"

Nikki takes off her pink hoodie. Gets on her knees. Wipes my bloody trail so the cops won't see where I went.

P's all questions in our apartment. "You a'ight? Can you move your fingers? Your hand feel broke? What if cops come in here . . . ? Should we run to the roof?"

I feel so many feelings I don't know how to answer. "You think Cole saw all the blood? He was shook. You think he good?"

"Yeah, he's fine. I saw him go in his house," P says. "*But your hand—*"

Nikki comes in and locks both locks. "The bathroom. Go rinse your hand."

As we go there, someone bangs on our door hard. "Is anyone home? This is the police!"

We three stand still. I think we're all holding our breath.

Then Nikki mouths, *Go. Quietly. Rinse.* She points to the bathroom.

I should be feeling pain but all I feel is fear. *If the cops come in here . . . we might all get locked up.*

"*Trev.*" Nikki's whisper jerks me. "Ma or Jess could come home now. If they let those cops in, the cops can't see blood."

I tiptoe to the bathroom with P and start rinsing, and my blood swirls in the drain.

I beef to P, "This is all Nikki's fault. If she didn't bring them here—"

P interrupts. "Wiggle your fingers."

I do.

"That hurt?"

"Nah." I exhale.

"Make a fist."

I do and P glad-sighs. "Your hand's good. You're lucky it's just cut."

Our apartment door bangs louder and I'm extra scared. "Nikki put us in this mess. That window's her fault. So is my hand. And now Cole's scared too."

I keep riffin' and P finally cuts me off me. "Bruh, you saw what you did?"

"What?"

"Remember we said, 'Hands solve stuff'?"

"Yeah."

"What you did was slick, Trev! You threw hands and showed Rick your power without hitting him. So him and his boys got the message. They know now that you'd knock them out. They won't mess with Nikki no more. Problem solved."

"Yeah? You think so?"

P nods. He seems so sure. But I wonder . . .

CHAPTER 48

THE cops stop knocking.

My stepdad's on my mind. Maybe since I feel like him? In trouble with 5-0 because of hands.

I think back to when P spoke, like stating an equation: *Sometimes you just gotta throw hands. Some cats don't get it, till they get hit.*

And again I hear my stepdad making me promise: *Don't let no one mess with your sisters. Protect them, no matter what.* Then he put up his fists. *With these.*

How it sounded—as if he had it all figured out—like one and one's two.

Throw hands. He gets the message. Then he stops his nonsense.

I stroke my knuckles, not knowing what to think.

Nikki comes in. "The cops left. They knocked on every apartment on our floor. No one opened."

"We lucky." I sigh.

Then she flips. "You an idiot."

"What? How me? My hand's busted because of you—"

"And I hope it's broke. How you get good grades, stupid? And that window? What you gonna tell Ma?"

What the—? How she's calling me stupid? How she's putting this on me?

None of this adds up.

Sometimes you gotta throw hands. That's facts. P knows it. My stepdad too. That's how it is here—everywhere. That stops nonsense.

But stuff doesn't feel solved. I feel like I'm the problem.

Did I cause the problem?

CHAPTER 49

MA walks in, confused. "There's glass in the hall. Someone broke the window—" She sees my hand and freezes. Then she comes to me and cups my fist in her hands.

Her moan. I heard her moan this way when my stepdad went away.

Nikki beasts before I can speak.

"So, Trev . . ."

Ugh. Nikki says only her side. Not facts.

"Hold up—" I try talking, but Nikki won't let me.

Ma's eyes stay on my hand. Her hurt face is worse than my hurt fist.

I just stand still, hoping it'll calm her.

Every word from Nikki stops having sound because I tune her out.

"Ma, I . . ."

Instead of her hearing me, she goes and sits. Sits in a sadness.

I want to yell but think that'll put us further in mess.

I don't know how to get us out of this. None of us know how to get out of it.

After a while, Mom finally speaks. "Explain the window."

I take a deep breath and then tell her everything.

"Where do you think using your hands this way will take you?"

When I don't answer, she does. "I'll tell you: where your stepdad is. What would've happened if the cops caught you? Do you think getting involved with the law is good? You got lucky this time, but what happens the next time?"

Next time? I don't want a next time.

I don't want Little Cole looking at me all confused. I'm not tryna make my sister be as shook as she was, thinking cops would snatch me. And how hurt Ma looked? Nah.

But then again, I can't just let people hurt my family. I want them to be safe—*and* . . . I don't know what to do.

CHAPTER 50

IN school, Ms. Clark sits in front of her smart board, looking back and forth from her laptop up to the big screen. She's focused-focused. I stand in the doorway and squint and see rows of headshots of famous people. Some dead, some alive. Lots I know.

I think, *She's in her zone. Maybe I should leave her alone—*

She looks over and our eyes meet. "Trevor! Come in. What's up?"

I feel bad for not working harder in this class. I feel bad I'm slipping, in school and out. I need words. I need someone. Something to help me not slip deeper into more messes.

I look down and spot a fidget spinner on her desk and point to it. "I was just thinking about those. They spin fast. But stay in one spot."

She notices the Band-Aids on my knuckles and I stuff my hand in my hoodie.

She pretends she didn't see my hand. This is another

way she shows she's cool. She keeps talking about the fidget spinner. "They do that."

"I feel that way sometimes."

"How?"

"Life is going on but I feel stuck."

Her nod says keep speaking.

Remember why you stopped by, I think to myself. Then I say, "Came to talk about something you said."

"What? When?"

I step in. "Promise. Remember you said I had it?"

"Of course! And you still do."

CHAPTER 51

"THANKS, Ms. Clark," I tell her. "I know I've been sleeping in class. I know I'm slipping. And I want to let you know it's because . . ." I feel it. I'm about to tell her everything. My stepdad in jail. Him hitting Ma. His promise. My promise. How I'll body him if he hits Ma again. "So there's another promise—one I made to my family."

Mad love is in her eyes. Worry too. Her look holds on to me. Holds me from leaving.

Ms. Clark asks, "You made a promise?"

"Yeah."

"Do you want to share it?"

"No."

"Do you want advice?"

"No."

She's studying my face, figuring out what to say.

Finally she speaks. "Okay, here's the thing with promises—as long as they don't hurt you, or anyone else, then they're okay to keep."

I nod.

"Trevor?"

"Yeah."

"Another thing—your promise shouldn't hurt *your* promise, your potential."

"I get that," I say and stand there, thinking about how I don't want to hurt *anybody*. I look back at her smart board and I recognize someone.

Words blurt out. "That's Muhammad Ali. Did you know he only counted his reps of an exercise once his muscles started to hurt."

Ms. Clark's impressed. "Where'd you learn that?"

"In the rec center in my neighborhood."

"Trevor, when I say you have 'promise,' I mean lots of things. You're a thinker and you ask good questions. You bring real-world learning into class. The way you just made Muhammad Ali even more interesting."

I joke, "Prolly got a lot more promise when I'm not sleeping."

Ms. Clark smiles. "Exactly," she says.

Then she turns serious. "Just let me know if there's anything I can do to help you not be so tired. Remember, I'm here for you whenever you want to talk."

CHAPTER 52

AFTER school, I just want to escape but can't. Glass is still on my hall floor. Saw it this morning. You'd think housing workers would clean it up, but housing barely does its job, ever.

On the train, my mind sees the glass. *I gotta fix that mess. Don't want Little Cole stepping in it.*

Getting off the train, my mind is on the glass. *I gotta make the hall spotless.*

Walking home, my mind is on the glass. *Will the hall still be quiet with that busted window?*

When I get to my block, I stop because cops are near my stoop.

I slow up.

Then I see one of the cops wave a teen over and point at the window. The teen shrugs.

All day my mood's been an elevator on its way down, and now it drops straight to the basement with no brakes.

I don't know where to go or what to do. I just know I need to escape.

I U-turn and leave before 5-0 see me.

I don't feel like myself.

On the edge of my projects, it hits me. I wonder if this is how my stepdad felt when cops came for him.

I walk faster. Don't want nothing reminding me of my stepdad. Don't want to feel like him.

Maybe I could just keep walking. Leave the projects for good. Walk out of my life. Train station comes into sight. Maybe I can ride it somewhere. Go someplace. I don't know.

Near the station, a shout spins me around. "Trev!"

Uncle Larry's street ESP is on and knows something's up from how I swung around. He lifts his hands in I-come-in-peace style. "Whoa, Trev."

Just seeing him, my whole everything feels lighter, different, better. He's the uncle I most need to see because he's the opposite of most men I know . . . plus, he escaped.

CHAPTER 53

"**YOU** look glad to run into me." Uncle Larry fist-bumps me. "But I'm maybe more glad to run into you."

"Why?"

"Because you the best person to answer a question I have."

"Okay."

"Trev, you saw *Black Panther*, right?"

I nod. "Wakanda forever."

He smiles. "I'ma try a dating app and might describe myself as T'Challa-looking. Chadwick Boseman and I got similarities, right?"

My laugh busts out before I can answer. Dang, it feels good to laugh. "Uncle, only if T'Challa was a tall NBA player."

He squats a little. "How 'bout now?"

"Sure," I say, laughing more.

"Trev, we need more movies like *that*."

"More Black Panther movies?"

"No. I mean, yeah, but more than *Black Panther*. Movies with *us*. Set in another world."

"Us?"

"Us-us. People who look like us. Showing us in other worlds."

Other worlds, I think, sounds good.

Uncle Larry says, "Films used to be all white. Like the original Star Wars movies. Love them but they too white-white." He sees I don't know what he means.

"Trev, you saw them first ones, right?"

"Nah. Just the new ones."

"What? You never saw *Empire Strikes Back* or *Return of the Jedi?*"

"Nope."

"You got to—they're the joints."

"Joints?"

"The jam."

"Jam?"

"Ugh. You youngins say 'lit.' 'Tight.' Trev, them Star Wars are lit, tight, even though they could have used more people of color. Hey, you free now?"

"Yeah."

Uncle Larry checks in with Ma, and of course she says yes since she loves me being with him.

All of a sudden my day's flipped. I'll be in Uncle Larry's Harry Potter library-apartment, and it's always an escape into another world. Plus, we'll see an original Star Wars movie? What?! That's an escape on top of an escape.

CHAPTER 54

ON the way, Uncle Larry points at a store. "Let's get some candies. It's not a full movie experience without them, right? My treat."

We cross the street toward the bodega and a guy even thinner than Larry calls to him, "Oye, flaco."

Huh? In Spanish that means "skinny" and this man's the one built like a broomstick.

But Larry gives him a thumbs-up and winks. My stepdad would've maybe threw hands with Mr. Broomstick and swept the floor with him. Larry can take a joke and ignore disses.

Inside the store, Uncle nods. "Trev, get whatev."

At first I don't because Ma taught us, *Don't be greedy.*

He notices that and shrugs. "You won't? I will." He starts grabbing trash candies.

"No, Uncle. Them are nasty."

He laughs and puts the trash candy back. "Fine. *Now* will you pick?"

I point. "Plain M&MS."

He grabs them. "And?"

"Twizzlers."

He takes those too.

"Airheads and Snickers, for sure."

He pays and I feel like a little-little kid again. Someone is taking care of me. I feel Little-Cole-good with no problems.

CHAPTER 55

AT his apartment, Uncle Larry holds an open box in front of me. "Which movie? *Star Wars? Empire? Return of the Jedi?*"

I lift one up. "*Return of the Jedi.* This title's fire."

The movie starts and it's us being jokey. Every now and then we pause the movie to silly-react to *whoa* scenes. He's *so* good at making Star Wars movie sounds. "*Swsssh!*" He lifts a straw like a light saber, stands up, and starts dueling the air.

I feel myself smiling. Uncle Larry knows how to cheer me up.

"Uncle, your voices are good."

"Thanks. Listen to this and tell me who I am now?"

Yo, his Darth Vader voice?! He sounds *just like* Vader!

My cell vibrates and I pull it out. It's P. He's my boy, but I just want to be here chilling now, so I stuff my cell back in my pocket.

"Trev, I have the Force." Unc points at a Snickers. "Watch me move that."

I cock my head at him. "You gonna move that?"

"Shh." He bites his lip, grunting. *"Focus, Larry,"* he tells himself in his Yoda voice.

I fold my arms. The candy sits there.

I lean in and grab it—"Here, Uncle"—handing it to him.

He laughs. "See? I made it move. I got the Force!"

CHAPTER 56

WE watch more, and during a Yoda scene I elbow Uncle. "Ma's my Yoda."

He busts out laughing.

"What's so funny?!" I ask.

"Ooh, I'm *telling* on you! I'm telling your mother you said she looks like Yoda."

I give him a look. "Don't play. That's *not* what I said."

When he sees I'm serious, he nods. "I know. They're both wise in this gentle way."

"Yeah. Exactly. They give good advice."

"Mm-hmm, they sure do."

Soon, we're back to watching the movie and having more fun.

But soon the fun stops because this movie starts reminding me of my life. Luke Skywalker squares up to fight his dad, Darth Vader.

I ask, "Hold up. Is Luke really gonna fight his pops?"

"Yeah," he says. "And it's one of the best scenes. *Watch.*"

I watch and feel like I'm staring at my future. It's me in danger, not Luke. I try hiding my reaction to this scene. "Unc, pause. You want more popcorn?"

He points. "Popcorn bowl's full."

"I meant soda. Want more?"

"Trev"—he points at our cups—"they full."

"I need to pee."

Uncle presses Pause. His street ESP scans my face. "Trev, this scene bugging you?"

I thumb my cracked knuckles. "Uncle? Just tell me, Luke wins, right?"

He eyes my knuckles. "What if he doesn't?"

I scoot to the edge of my seat and sit straight. "Then I might not want to see this."

He breathes out deep. "You Luke?"

I'm so east and west that I shake my head a no, then nod a yes.

"That makes sense, Trev."

"Huh, why?"

"Cuz your stepdad's Darth Vader."

I stay quiet. He is, *for real.*

"You feel you have to fight him? Is that why your knuckles are torn up?"

I shove my fists in my hoodie.

Uncle Larry presses. "Why your fists bruised?"

I sit back. Tired of holding it all in. "Uncle, can we talk-talk?"

CHAPTER 57

I tell Uncle Larry about my stepdad getting out of jail next month and his promise to hurt Ma.

"You plan to fight him?" Uncle Larry guesses.

"Yeah. That's why I've been working out. Getting stronger so I can protect Ma."

"Real talk, Trev? Your mom is strong. Stronger than him and most out here."

"What?"

"You know the Jedi have the Force? Well, your mom *is* a force. She takes care of you three kids. She didn't stay hit the last time your stepdad hit her, did she? Calling the cops takes strength. And now he's in jail. She's never been in jail—that takes strength too. Not that everyone in jail is weak. Not that everyone in jail did wrong. But she stays out of traps out here. And how she sees rainbows in us?"

"Yeah. She loves that quote."

"Choosing to be the rainbow takes strength—a different kind of strength."

I nod.

He keeps on. "Solving things with anger—the Darth Vader way—won't take the pain away. Won't take you to a good place. I bet you think about your stepdad so much it wears you out."

"It does."

"Yeah, because you're living in stress, in survival mode. Your mind's telling your body you're always in danger. I mean, look at you. You just were *so* kid-happy with candy and Star Wars. Then thinking of your stepdad, you flipped. Now you got bags under your eyes and look old as me. And I'm a hundred."

I chuckle. "A hundred."

Uncle Larry starts looking under the couch. "So, where's your stepdad?" He goes behind the TV. "Is he here?"

"Stop playing. You know he's in jail."

"Then don't let him stress you out if he ain't here. When he comes out, then your stepdad is real. But now? Who's keeping you in pain?"

Never thought of it that way. "Me?"

"Yes. *You.* You sitting in all this anger. Your stepdad's in jail but you kinda in jail too. Using your hands to fight? That's just imitating him. Soon, your life'll be an imitation of his. And all of us don't want that for you. Forget him. Let me and other people help."

CHAPTER 58

ON the way back home from Uncle Larry's, I think about him saying *All of us*, and I flash back to when Uncle Frankie said my parents' fight wasn't his business. That got me tight. So did my school's banner: IT TAKES A VILLAGE TO RAISE A CHILD.

But maybe I do have a village.

I wonder who here helps me avoid traps? Who wants me to be me? *Not* my stepdad.

All these faces start popping up in my mind. Nikki. Jess. Ma. Ms. Clark. My uncles. Quick from the rec.

I guess a lot of people really do have my back.

CHAPTER 59

WHEN I get near our building, P's waiting for me.

"Where you been?" I say. "Let's go to the stadium."

His face ain't right. Something's wrong.

"Cops came to our place, so I peeled. Was at my uncle Larry's."

"I know cops came, Trev! They *caught* me."

"What?!" My fists clench from hearing cops cornered him. "What happened, P?"

"They musta been milling around our building's halls all day. They caught me before I could jet. Hit me with all these questions." He replays it.

> Cops: "This window. You know about it?"
>
> P: "No."
>
> Cops: "How no? You live here?"
>
> P: "I don't know why it's broke, officers."
>
> Cops: "You sure? Like how sure?"

P goes real silent.

"My bad. I got you in this mess."

Now I feel worser than worse.

CHAPTER 60

"**TOO** bad your pops isn't around," P says. "He woulda handled Rick on day one. And you wouldn't have had to bust that window to scare him off. Your pops is a Leo. Lions defend their own."

"You think he has heart?"

"Yeah. And he's nice with hands too."

I hate that P is praising my stepdad. I've held back the truth from him for a while. Right now, I'm tired of doing that. "About my pops's hands, you know why he's in jail?"

"A fight?"

I grit my teeth. "For hitting my moms."

"What the—?! That's foul!"

"She had to call the cops on him. Had to. Bruh, he— I feel so—" All these feelings are taking over me. I turn to hide my face because I never cried in front of P before.

I try to stop but can't, and tears come out.

I see him out the side of my eye. P doesn't know what to do. He's froze.

I low-growl. "My pops isn't the Man. He's *not*! You think he has heart?! Heart means you care too."

"Yeah," P agrees.

"And let him be foul around me again"—I pump my fist—"he'll know how it feels to get hit."

"You can't fight your pops. I mean, you probably could. But, what if . . ."

I shrug-sniff. "Don't matter. Sometimes you gotta throw hands. *You* said that."

"This won't turn out right."

"It don't matter what happens to me. I can't let him put his hands on my moms."

"Trev, you got time to figure it out. When's your pops out?"

I wipe snot. "This month. Maybe I got a couple weeks." The feeling I have, I don't want to speak. "Can we just not talk?"

We just sit. The sun sets.

As the sky's colors fade, my cheeks dry.

CHAPTER 61

AT home, Nikki pokes her head in my door. "Can we talk?"

I shrug.

"You stupid," she says.

"You stupider!"

"But you the stupidest."

We both laugh and she sits next to me. "I'm sorry."

"You really came to say sorry?"

"Yeah."

"Did Ma tell you to say sorry to me? Or Jess?"

"Nah. No one. Trev"—Nikki looks at me with real honest eyes—"I know you were just tryna protect me. Maybe you right—maybe I *am* stupid."

"Why you say that?"

"Because instead of thinking, I followed my heart. I hate to say it, but Jess was right—Rick doesn't really care about me. I brought someone into our family who hurt us. And we already got someone in the family hurting us, right?"

"Well, at least you know now." I nudge Nikki.

We fight, but we have each other's back.

CHAPTER 62

LATE at night I lie in bed and stare at my posters of Creed about to fight, then at Muhammad Ali throwing a punch.

Muhammad Ali in the poster looks so strong in the right way.

Creed too.

But this throwing-hands stuff. Maybe it's not the way for me to go.

I threw hands and now I feel grimy I got P involved with 5-0. I feel bad I scared Little Cole. I feel . . . I don't know.

Because what did hands really do? Added up to things being off. I showed Rick I'm not playing. And so?

Did it stop nonsense?

Did it make him go away?

Now all these people are involved. Cops too. Is the problem solved?

I got Uncle Larry's voice in my head—Quick's and Uncle Frankie's too. They got me asking the same thing.

Why throw hands? When using my brain might be better. And throwing hands turns me into my stepdad.

Except I don't know what else to do.

All these feelings have me shook up like a soda can about to explode. It's bedtime and I can't sleep. And if I do, I'll probably have the same nightmare again.

"Forget it." I huff-snatch the sheet off me, get on the floor, and start banging out push-ups. I get up and flex my arm. My bicep muscle is a softball. But in my heart, I feel like a dry leaf. One squeeze and *crunch*, I'll crumple. I feel so east and west. I can't face my stepdad in a dream this way. Nah. I do more push-ups. Figure I'll work out until I can't. Soon, I lie down in my bed, huffing.

Huffing . . .

. . . until I melt into my pillow.

CHAPTER 63

SIRENS *flash and my eyes pop open. How am I outside?*

Buildings light up on my packed block.

Wait. Details here don't make sense. Ant's a neighborhood kid who died a year ago, but he's here? Ms. Louise's family moved. They here. Then I realize it: I'm dreaming. I'm reliving my stepdad getting locked up. But where's he at?

I look around and see Ma, my sisters. How come they so far away? Why they frowning sadder than I remember?

I yell, "It's okay. Pa's in the cop car! He can't hurt us! Don't be sad. Be glad."

Only thing: No sound comes out. How? I shout again. Nothing. Comes. Out. Then I hear a man say my last name. Then I see it: I'm in the cop car.

The cop grins, repeating my name. "Like father, like son. I arrested your father. Now you."

"This is a mistake!" I yell. "And he's not my father!"

The cop shakes his head.

I look out at Ma. She's crying now.

I want to hug her but I can't. I shift, and keys jingle on my lap. No, not keys—chains. My bloody fists are in cuffs. How—? What happ—?

P's voice next to me scares me. "Sometimes you gotta throw hands."

"P, why you in this back seat too? Why you in cuffs?!"

He repeats, "Sometimes you gotta throw hands." Like a robot adding. Like one plus one is two.

"But, P, none of this adds up right. We arrested."

Both cops in the front laugh. "It's how it is. Like father. Like son."

"NO! I'm not my dad!" I yell. "At least let my friend go!"

The cop car's tires crunch. They drive me and P off my block. "No!!!"

The sirens keep flashing.

Our buildings keep lighting up, a burning color.

A shape I didn't see before is near Ma. My stepdad! His eye is swollen and his face is a little bruised. Did I do that?

He stands behind Ma.

I yell, "Ma, Jess, Nikki! You not safe!" But I have no voice.

My stepdad grins, wrapping an arm around Ma. He has her right in his hands.

CHAPTER 64

"**HURRY** for school," Ma tells me.

I'm moving mad slow in my room, dead tired from the night before.

Plus I'm trying to wait for my sisters to leave, so it'll just be Ma and me. I don't even know what I want to say to her. I just . . . She's the only one I can talk to and not seem soft. *Gentle giant*, she calls me. She'll let me express myself.

I wait.

Jess heads out. Nikki is getting ready to go.

"Love you." Nikki kisses Ma and leaves. I come into the living room.

"You're going to be late, Trev. Rush."

I swallow and sit. "Ma?" My tone makes her eyes snap to me. "Ma . . . I . . . I . . . Can we talk?"

She comes and sits next to me.

There's a storm of emotions in me, and I can't lightning-bolt her with all my feelings. I don't know where to start, so I ask her, "You ever want to move?"

She shifts, looks uncomfortable. She gives me a look, so soft. "Why?"

I could name a million reasons. But I mumble the main one. "To get away from *him*. My stepdad."

"Your stepdad?"

"He promised some messed-up stuff when he went back to jail. Remember?"

Ma's face is shocked. "I won't let anything happen to us, Trev."

I rub my cracked, bloody knuckles and think of every nightmare I've had. "If he hurts you, I'll—"

She grabs my hands. "Stop."

"He doesn't deserve you, Ma. We all worried—Jess and Nikki too."

Ma strokes my hands. "The last thing I want is you three worrying."

"Well, we are. I am."

"Trev, I've been thinking a lot about this too. But for now, just know that I'll do what's best for you and your sisters. It'll be all right. I promise."

CHAPTER 65

LITTLE Cole is in my hall when I come home from school, and he's sweating a little.

"Hi, Trevor, watch this," he tells me, then throws sloppy punches in the air.

"What you doing?"

He points at the broken window. "You're so strong. I want to be that strong."

I can't believe he's admiring me for breaking that window—for something I don't want props for.

I don't want Cole fighting. All of a sudden I want to tell him things my uncles told me about not fighting. My mind rewinds to Ma telling me I'm a good influence on him.

"Cole, wait right here."

"Okay."

I go in my apartment and come out with white copy paper and colored pencils from the sneaker box with my drawings—pencils I used when I was his age.

"Cole, let's sit. You want hand skills? I'ma show you

how to be *nice* with your hands. Want to learn how to shade a character's face so you can see their emotions?"

"Yeah!"

And then I do what I haven't done since I was maybe eight. I sit crisscross-applesauce in our hallway and start to draw. "Okay, master artist, first you do this . . ."

I notice Cole's face is into it–into it.

We may only be drawing, but this moment feels like so much more. Like real power.

CHAPTER 66

THE next day I'm walking to the store when loud rap beats from a car spin me around. It's Uncle Puff cruising up. "Trev, hop in. Check out the new stuff I had installed in my car."

I get in.

"First feature"—he points at his car's radio—"play whatever."

I pick a rap song I like, and as it plays, the floor's LEDs light up with a different bright color each time the beat changes.

"Wow! This is wild how these lights follow the rhythm of the song."

He nods. "Yep. Bust this other feature," and he rolls up his tinted windows and presses a button. It goes almost dark-dark in here and the buttons on the dashboard glow a cool electric blue. With that and the lights on the floor flowing with the music, we might as well be in a club I see on music videos, except on wheels.

He raises the volume, the beat gets harder, and me and him start bopping our heads to the music, and I tap my hands on his dashboard to the rhythm. Driving and bopping and rapping and . . . my mind just shuts off and it feels good to get lost in this zone.

Minutes pass, then Puff stops his car and turns down the music.

"Where we at?" I ask, and he lowers his tinted windows.

We're outside Uncle Frankie's garage.

I eye Puff. "Why you bring me here?"

"Frankie asked me to." He shrugs. "Didn't say why but he's family—he's been good to you since you was a baby. So talk to him, cool?"

I tell Puff, "Yeah. It's all good." The way I feel? Stuff's happened since me and Frankie last spoke. Stuff that makes me think that maybe I should hear him out.

Frankie comes out of his garage toward us.

"You want me to stay parked here?" Puff asks.

"Nah, Uncle. I'll walk home after."

Puff and Frankie throw each other peace signs, and Uncle Puff drives off.

CHAPTER 67

ME and Frankie stand face-to-face, look in each other's eyes, and without speaking, we both start heading into his garage at the same time.

Stepping into his office, everything is the same. Plants all over. His car seat–couch with coils sticking out. Everything's the same except how I feel. I don't feel like that little day care boy anymore—safe and protected by him. I want to sit on that car seat–couch and feel that way but I can't. I stay standing.

Uncle Frankie interrupts my thinking. "There's some things I want to say to you."

"Maybe there's some things I want to say to you."

"So? Who first?"

I nod at him. "You can go."

He sits behind his desk. "Your uncle Lou—your mom's brother, rest his soul—is my brother forever. And I got to thinking, Lou wanted different for you. But how you gonna be different if you don't have help?"

I nod.

He pounds his fist to his heart. "I'ma help—with your stepdad."

I'm glad he said that. I go sit on the couch while asking, "You sure?"

"Trev, I'll have your back—your mom's and sisters' too. We'll figure it out together."

"Uncle"—the words come flowing out—"I was mad the last time I left here. On the way home, I saw this sign outside my school—something about how we a village—and I didn't agree then. When you said my parents' situation wasn't your business, that made me wonder if I had a village. But I feel different now, like I do have a village."

"Yeah, you do. And I'm part of it. We got your back. I promise."

"Thanks." All the things people told me and all the stuff that happened since I was last here in this garage starts popping up in my head.

"Uncle, I been thinking, and you might be right about how jumping into one mess is gonna make more messes. Been thinking about that and how I need to keep my promises to the right people. I don't have it all figured out, but I feel better knowing I have help."

"You got it, Trev." Uncle Frankie grabs two sodas from his fridge and holds one out for me.

I take it, pop it open, sip, and the bubbles make me burp.

We start to laugh, and sitting here, smiling, I start to feel it again.

Like I'm cared for, with a village looking out for me.

I feel . . . not stuck . . . like the future could be full of promises I want.

Like I know I got choices and people who'll help me make the right ones.

I eye the napkin taped to the wall in Uncle's handwriting: *Be a rainbow in someone's cloud.*

Yeah, I think. *Yeah.*

ACKNOWLEDGMENTS

Charlotte, Nancy! You and our agency family and imprint family are the best!

Ma, you're gone but not forgotten. You died this year on National Spider-Man Day, and it fits. "With great power comes great responsibility." You taught me that there's great power in books, and I feel a responsibility to share *Hands*. Why? For starters, when I was Trevor's age, I wish someone handed me *Hands*. I needed it how many of my students need it now. As an adolescent, I felt Trevor's ups and downs, but while writing *Hands*, I felt more up than down, so I hope this book also helps readers feel more up and figure out how to feel less down. When we feel weighed down, we don't need a book heavy in page count or content to weigh us down more. So *Hands* aims to be fast-paced and thin, yet thick with complexity. My fingers are crossed that *Hands* empowers anyone experiencing similar issues to respond to challenges in ways that keep empowering them and others.

To my daughter and wife, you are at the top of the list with Ma as the best family. I love you.

Speaking of family, this book reminds us family isn't just who is blood related—family is who stays awhile and does the most in each letter of F.R.I.E.N.D.S. So, if you're blood or not and you stay doing the following, I appreciate that you:

Fight for me

Respect me

Involve me

Encourage me

Nurture me

Develop me

Stand by me.

Finally, all of you who told me you couldn't wait for this, my next book, filled my heart with happiness and fuel to write. There are so many of you that if I start naming each of you, this acknowledgments section will become a whole other book! I thank you ALL.